KU-708-243

Read alone

The class go to the seaside.
Bumpy hides in the picnic basket.

When the class arrive at the beach, Osbourne and Harriet unpack the picnic basket and all the towels, rubber rings, armbands, buckets and spades!

Bumpy crawls out of the basket, towards the beach. Nobody sees him wriggle along the sand.

Harriet puts sun cream and a sun hat on everyone before they go off to play. Timmy puts a sun hat on Teddy and holds him tightly. **Booh!**

Read alone

Timmy must keep Teddy safe.
No one sees Bumpy crawl away.

Yabba, Stripey, Mittens and Timmy
put on their rubber rings and armbands
and play in the sea. Timmy makes sure Teddy
wears a rubber ring too. **Splish! Splash!
Splosh!**

But Mittens doesn't like getting wet.
Mee-eew! Harriet has another
idea. She calls the friends out of the
water and gives them each a bucket
and spade to play with.

Harriet shows Mittens how to collect
shells in her bucket.

Read alone

Timmy and Teddy play in the sea with their friends.

Read aloud   Read along

Harriet lies down on the beach and gets Timmy and his friends to cover her in sand. They use their spades to plop sand onto Harriet's tummy and feet.

Timmy sits Teddy safely down on the beach as he digs. **Baah! Baah!** This is fun!

Timmy sees a clump of seaweed nearby, and puts it on his head, making everybody laugh.

Bumpy has been playing under the seaweed. He quickly hides in the sand.

Read alone

The friends cover Harriet in sand.
Bumpy hides under some seaweed.

Nearby, Otus is building a sandcastle. Timmy collects his bucket and comes to help him. Timmy sits Teddy out of the way so he won't get sand in his fur.

Otus is worried that Timmy will knock his castle over. But it's OK – Timmy, very carefully, builds a tower on the top.

Otus picks up his bucket to make more towers. Bumpy has been hiding underneath it. He wriggles away before Otus sees him!

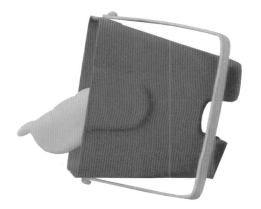

Read alone

Timmy and Otus build a sandcastle.
Bumpy hides under a bucket.

Read aloud   Read along

Suddenly Timmy hears a **WHUSH! WHUSH! WHUSH!** Osbourne is inflating a red boat, called a dinghy. Timmy helps to pump up the boat until it's full of air. Teddy helps, too.

But Osbourne accidentally knocks the pump over. The air whooshes out, the dinghy flies off and it deflates like a giant balloon! **PFFFF!**

Poor Osbourne has to chase the dinghy and pump it up all over again!

Read alone

Osbourne inflates a big boat.
Timmy and Teddy try to help.

Just then, Harriet rings the bell to tell everyone it's lunchtime. Timmy makes sure Teddy has a place on his picnic blanket.

Mittens sits with her bucket of shells. Suddenly she gives a loud squeal. **Mee-eew!** Her bucket is moving by itself.

Mittens is scared. But brave Timmy looks inside the bucket and finds Bumpy hiding under a shell! What a surprise!

Read alone

At lunch, Timmy sits next to Mittens.
He finds Bumpy in her bucket!

Read aloud   Read along

After lunch, Ruffy and Finlay dig
a moat. It fills with seawater. Timmy thinks
that looks like fun. **Booh!** He digs another
moat from Otus' sandcastle down to the sea.
Then he builds Teddy a wooden raft.

Timmy sits Teddy on the raft while he helps
decorate the sandcastle with seashells. He sees
a big, shiny shell and runs to show Osbourne.

But this time, Timmy forgets about Teddy,
and leaves him behind
on the raft.

Read alone

Ruffy and Finlay dig a moat. Timmy builds a raft for Teddy to sit on.

Read aloud Read along

Bumpy finds Teddy on his raft and wriggles on board. Teddy's furry tummy is so comfortable that Bumpy falls asleep!

Suddenly, the tide comes in and water **WHOOSHES** up to the moat. Teddy and Bumpy are swept out to sea!

Meanwhile, Osbourne shows Timmy how to hold the conch shell to his ear to hear the sea. Timmy runs back to tell Teddy and his friends what he's learnt. **Baah!**

Read alone

Bumpy falls asleep on Teddy's raft.
The tide washes them out to sea!

But Teddy is nowhere to be seen!
Booh! Timmy is very worried and upset.
Where has Teddy gone?

Meanwhile, Bumpy wakes up, and is shocked
to find that he and Teddy are sailing out
to sea! **Eek!**

Then Bumpy spots something
else floating on the water nearby.
It's a bottle! That gives
Bumpy an idea ...

Read alone

Timmy can't find Teddy.
He is very worried and upset!

Bumpy writes a message. Then he puts it in the bottle and throws it back into the sea. He hopes someone finds it soon!

The bottle floats towards the beach and into the moat, where Yabba sees it. **Quack!** She watches the bottle as it floats along to where Timmy sits on the sand.

Read alone

Bumpy sends for help. Yabba sees
Bumpy's message in a bottle.

Read aloud   Read along

Timmy takes the message out of the bottle. There is a picture on it, showing Teddy and Bumpy on their raft out at sea. **Booh!** They need help!

Timmy has to rescue Teddy and Bumpy. And he knows exactly how to do it! He just needs to borrow the big, red dinghy ...

Read alone

Timmy knows where Teddy is!
He has to rescue his little friends.

Osbourne and Timmy put on lifejackets, grab a pair of oars and jump into the dinghy. **Hoot hoot! Booh!**

Timmy to the rescue!

Teddy and Bumpy drift further out to sea and Osbourne has to paddle harder and harder to get close to them! Harriet and the class watch the rescue from the beach. It's very exciting but a little bit scary too!

Read alone

Timmy sails out to sea. The class are worried as the raft drifts away.

Suddenly the little raft
is in sight. Ship ahoy! **Baah!**

Timmy throws a rope towards Teddy
and Bumpy, but it misses the raft. Timmy
tries again. This time, the rope nearly knocks
Teddy overboard!

The next time, Bumpy catches the rope in his
mouth and ties it to the raft. Osbourne rows
them all back to shore. Timmy
gives his two little friends
a big cuddle. **Baah!**

The whole class is
pleased to see Timmy,
Bumpy and Teddy
safe at last!

Read alone

Timmy throws a rope and Bumpy catches it. Now they are safe again!

Read aloud   Read along

It's soon time for the class to go home. It's been a very exciting day!

Osbourne loads everything back onto the roof rack. This time, though, Bumpy doesn't hide inside the picnic basket. He sits proudly next to Timmy on the back seat of the bus.

Teddy sits on Timmy's other side, safe and sound. Timmy won't let him out of his sight again!

Read alone

It's time to go home. Timmy keeps Teddy and Bumpy safe beside him!

Sign up today!

RECEIVED 03 SEP 2012

Monthly Catchup

children's books . mags . eBooks . apps

Does your child love books?

Register for Egmont's monthly e-newsletters and access our wonderful world of characters for **FREE!**

Catchup is packed with sneak previews of new books including much-loved favourites like Mr. Men, Thomas, Ben 10, Fireman Sam and loads more. Plus you'll get **special offers, competitions** and **freebies galore.**

SIGN UP TODAY FOR EXCITING NEWS STRAIGHT TO YOUR INBOX

Head to **egmont.co.uk** to register your details (at the top of the home page) and look out for **Catchup** in your inbox.

Get a whopping 35% off your first order! So you don't miss out on special offers, freebies and prize, add this email to your address book.

Monthly Catchup*

children's books . mags . eBooks . apps

EGMONT

Hello,

You haven't heard from us in a while. It's not because we've forgotten all about you! We've just been working on some brand-new ways to keep you updated about our exciting books. Once a month you can look forward to recieving our newsletter: Catchup. It'll be jam-packed with really interesting stuff like, what we've been up to, sneak previews to new books including much-loved favourites like Mr. Men, Thomas, Ben 10 and Fireman Sam, as well as news about brand-new characters and books. You'll also get updates from our magazine team, special offers, competitions and freebies galore.

Stuff to do 'n' win

Signed Mr. Tickle to give away...

Thomas the Tank Engine

Zhu-niverse™ here we come!

ZhuZhu Pets® have

Next month...

Sssh don't tell anyone but...

All About Bin Weevils Magazine Launching

All new special Bin Weevils magazine, on sale October 5th! It includes 7 amazing free gifts, comics, puzzles, posters, game tips and hints and a lot more.

All About Bin Weevils Magazine Launching

follow on Twitter | forward to a friend

So you don't miss out on special offers, freebies and prize, please add this email to your address book.

E1238